For Nina, with love — JN

For family and friends; the best fans a girl could have — DB

First published in hardback in Great Britain by HarperCollins Publishers Ltd in 2001
First published in paperback by Collins Picture Books in 2002

5 7 9 10 8 6 4
ISBN: 978 0 00 664766 9

Collins Picture Books is an imprint of the Children's Division, part of HarperCollins Publishers Ltd.
Text copyright © Jenny Nimmo 2001
Illustrations copyright © Debbie Boon 2001

The HarperCollins website address is:
www.harpercollins.co.uk

Printed in China

Something
Wonderful

Written by Jenny Nimmo Illustrated by Debbie Boon

HarperCollins *Children's Books*

Little Hen lived on a farm.

Mr and Mrs Field lived in the farmhouse.

Little Hen lived in the chicken house.

She lived with Lily and Biddie,

Rosie and Gertie and Arthur.

Lily and Biddie, Rosie and Gertie had all won prizes.

Little Hen had never won a prize. She asked Lily and Biddie,

Rosie and Gertie how they had won their prizes.

"We are special," they said. "We have special names."

"How can I be special?" asked Little Hen.

RHODE ISLAND RED

SILVER LACE

"You can't," they said. "You are too small and ordinary."

Little Hen was very sad.

Mrs Field was worried about Little Hen. She looked so forlorn.

"Don't be sad because you're small," said Mrs Field. "Small creatures can do wonderful things. Look at spiders."

Little Hen thought, I am not a spider. But she felt better all the same.

In the chicken house that night, Little Hen said, "I'm going to do

SOMETHING WONDERFUL."

"You?" cried the other hens. "Don't be silly." And they all fell about laughing.

HA HA HA HAHAHAHAHA**HA!**

Arthur didn't laugh.

The next day it was very hot in the farmyard.

One by one the hens went into the wood. They all laid their eggs in the same shady nest. And then they forgot them.

"Who's going to take care of the eggs?" called Little Hen. But none of them heard her.

That evening there were no eggs in the nesting box. And there was no Little Hen.

None of the hens knew where Little Hen was, and they had forgotten where they had laid their eggs.

"Little Hen is so silly," said Lily.

"She's probably got lost," said Biddie.

"I hope not," said Arthur.

"Where are the eggs for my tea?" asked Farmer Field.

"There are no eggs," said Mrs Field. "And Little Hen is missing."

"Oh dear," said Farmer Field. "She must have got lost."

That night there was a **TERRIBLE STORM**.

The hens heard the thunder and the rain.

"Silly Little Hen," said Rosie. "She'll get wet."

"Perhaps she'll drown," said Gertie.

"I wish she'd come back," said Arthur.

But Little Hen didn't come back.

The next evening Mrs
Field found four eggs in
the nesting box.

"Good girls," she told
the hens. But she missed
Little Hen.

Farmer Field had two eggs for his tea, but Mrs Field couldn't eat.

"Little Hen hasn't come back yet," she said.

"Oh dear," said Farmer Field, "Perhaps she drowned in the storm."

That night there was a **GREAT WIND.**

The hens heard the wind.

"Silly Little Hen," said Lily.

"She's so small, she'll blow away," said Biddie.

"I miss her," said Arthur.

Many days went by. Little Hen didn't come back.
Mrs Field made lots of cakes, but she wasn't happy.

One sunny day in the nest in the wood, something began to happen.

She walked out of the wood, across the field and into the farmyard.

Mrs Field jumped for joy and ran to tell Farmer Field.

"Five new chicks!" she said.

Lily and Biddie and Rosie and Gertie said nothing at all.

"Look what I've done!" cried Little Hen.

"Little Hen, you've done **SOMETHING WONDERFUL**," said Arthur.

And he gave Little Hen her very own special prize.